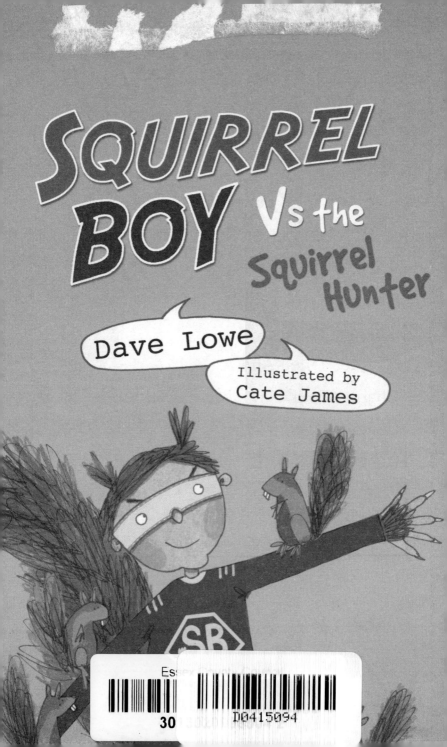

SQUIRREL BOY Vs the Squirrel Hunter

Dave Lowe

Illustrated by
Cate James

CONTENTS

Squirrel Boy vs the Squirrel Hunter

ISBN: 978-1-907-912-73-3

Published in the UK by Phoenix Yard Books Ltd
This edition published 2015

Phoenix Yard Books
Phoenix Yard
65 King's Cross Road
London
WC1X 9LW

1 3 5 7 9 10 8 6 4 2

Printed and bound by CPI Group (UK) Ltd, Croydon, CR0 4YY

A CIP catalogue record for this book is available from the British Library

www.phoenixyardbooks.com

For Heidi; the Very Special Delivery.

CHAPTER ONE

Have you ever noticed how some dog owners are exactly like their dogs?

The Box family, for example, have a labrador called Porky, who is so lazy that he can't be bothered chasing cats: he just glares at them and hopes they get the message. The Box family are just as lazy: they spend an awful lot of time glued to the TV. Even getting up from the sofa to go to the toilet seems like a huge hassle.

Jack Gunderson's Jack Russell, Russell,

on the other hand, is too lively. He can't stop yapping, and neither, for that matter, can Jack Gunderson himself: he talks to everyone he meets and goes on endlessly about the same three boring subjects:

1. the weather
2. how much better things used to be in the old days, and
3. how much better the weather used to be in the old days.

But this story isn't about Jack Gunderson, or the Boxes.

Which is very lucky, because a story about the Boxes would be very boring indeed. Nothing would happen at all, apart from them eating, burping, scratching and watching the telly. And a story about Jack Gunderson would just be him banging on and on about how rainy it's been; or how, when he was a kid, you could go to the movies for a few pennies, have a box of popcorn the size of a small building, and still have enough change left over to buy a medium-sized country.

No, this story is – at least partly – about a man called Auberon Steyn, and his dog, Snarl.

As you might guess by the name, Snarl isn't one of those cute little fluffy puppies that sits in your lap and licks your face.

Snarl is much too big for anyone's lap. And he isn't a licker.

Oh, no.

He's a biter.

And as for his owner, Auberon Steyn, he is small and podgy, he waddles when he walks, and he's quite possibly the most horrible man in the entire town.

CHAPTER TWO

There is no nice way to say this: Auberon Steyn liked killing things.

In Africa, there are men called 'Big-Game Hunters'. These are men with very big guns and very small brains, who think it's fun to shoot incredible beasts such as lions and elephants and cheetahs – animals who have done absolutely nothing to them – and mount the dead animals' heads on plaques, or make rugs out of their fur, and use them to decorate their big, stupid houses.

In the town where Auberon Steyn lived there were no lions or elephants or anything like that. But that didn't stop him from hunting things.

Auberon Steyn was a Small-Game Hunter.

He caught badgers and bunnies and birds. Any wild animal that moved – and some, like hedgehogs, that hardly moved at all – were fair game for Auberon Steyn.

But the animal he took the most pleasure in killing was the squirrel.

His house was full of trophies, but not trophies as you and I would know them. His trophies were not made of metal; they were badger heads on plaques, hedgehog -quill toothpicks and, most of all, squirrel tails. Hundreds of them, lining his walls.

The only animal that he could tolerate

– the only one in the entire world - was Snarl, an Alsatian with a short temper, a long piercing howl, and sharp teeth dripping with drool.

And it wasn't just animals that Auberon Steyn hated: he didn't think much of people, either; especially people who knocked on his door and disturbed him.

Not many people knocked on his door, of course. It wasn't the most inviting of houses, with an unruly front garden, dreary walls and drab curtains. Most of the neighbours kept well clear of Auberon Steyn and his dog.

One person who didn't know about him was Angela Kettle. Here she was, with a clipboard in her hand, making her way through the overgrown grass and weeds of the front garden up to the black front door.

When she knocked, Snarl started barking angrily and so loudly that the house seemed to rattle. Auberon Steyn had been skinning squirrels in his kitchen (he used the meat for pies). When he answered the door, he had blood on his hands and was still gripping the knife in his tight little fist.

"Yes?" he snapped, impatiently.

Angela's smile instantly disappeared when she saw the blood-smeared blade glinting in the man's hand and the wild look in the dog's eyes. She was a real animal lover, but there was something about this particular animal that looked ...well, unhinged.

"What do you want?" the man said, frowning.

"I'm here to collect signatures for Save the Tiger," she explained, showing him the clipboard.

"Save the Tiger?" he barked. "Why the devil would I want to do that?"

"Well," she said, calmly, "people are killing them for their fur, and there aren't so many tigers left in the wild these days. Soon there'll be none. They're truly magnificent animals. And they've been on this planet for many, many years..."

"Toothache!" the man spluttered.

"I'm sorry?" she said.

"Toothache," he repeated, "has also been around for many, many years. I don't suppose you have a petition trying to save that?"

"Well, no, but..."

"Those 'magnificent animals' that you are wittering on about; those stripy killers... Do you think that they care one jot about you or me? Do you think that they would sign a petition to Save the Person? Of course they wouldn't, even if they had pens. No. They'd bite off your head, Madam, as soon as look at you. Save the Tiger indeed! Kill the Tiger, now that's a petition I would gladly sign. Because the only good tiger, Madam, is a dead one. Now, shove off and leave me alone," he snapped, slamming the door in her face.

CHAPTER THREE

Let's leave Auberon Steyn to waddle back to the kitchen to make his disgusting squirrel-and-cabbage pies.

Instead, let's meet a much nicer person: a boy who lived about ten minutes' walk away, in a small, neat house with his mother.

This evening, while his mum was out collecting signatures for Save the Tiger, he was sitting in the front room belonging to their next-door neighbour, Mrs Onions. Whenever his mum went out, he had to go to Mrs Onions' place, so that she could 'look after' him, and he could help her out with some jobs around the house.

Walter didn't mind at all. Mrs Onions was an amazing cook and always plied him with delicious food and drink. And she would often regale him with tales of amazing adventures she'd had, all the while puffing on her pipe and filling the room with fragrant smoke. Also, and most importantly of all, she was the only person who knew his secret identity, and the only one he could talk to about those things:

Squirrel Boy things.

This evening, they were sitting quietly in her front room. She was reading the newspaper and puffing on her pipe. He was reading a Batman comic, munching on a home-made chocolate biscuit and washing it down with a glass of her delicious lemonade.

It was an ordinary front room, except for one detail: there were dozens of framed photos on the walls, and most of these were of Mrs Onions herself, sometimes with other people, sometimes alone. One glance around the room, and you'd know that she'd had a fantastically eventful life.

Mrs Onions looked up from the newspaper towards Walter, and coughed to get his attention. Well, she could have been coughing because of the pipe but, either way, it got his attention. He looked at her through the haze of smoke.

"I think I might have a job for Squirrel Boy," she said.

"Dusting again?" he asked. Sometimes she asked him to turn into a squirrel so he could use his tail (and his incredible climbing ability) to clean her high shelves. He didn't mind, though, not really.

"No," she said. "Crime-fighting."

He raised an eyebrow. She waved the newspaper at him.

"They've been at it again," she said.

"Who? At what?"

"Come with me," she said. She got up slowly from her armchair, hobbled out of the room and he followed her into the hall until they were at the door of the spare room. "I've been doing this room up all week," she said, proudly. "Welcome, young man, to SBHQ: Squirrel Boy Headquarters!"

When she pushed open the door, he was half-expecting to be dazzled by computer screens and hi-tech crime-fighting equipment. What he actually saw was a small table with two wooden chairs. Framed newspaper front pages of his exploits were hanging on the wall, next to a noticeboard that was filled with newspaper cuttings.

"Well?" she said. "What do you think?"

"It's not exactly the Batcave, is it?" he said.

"Take a seat at the Squirreltable," she said, ignoring him.

"It's just an ordinary table," he pointed out.

"But it's in Squirrel Boy HQ," she said, firmly, "which makes it very much the *Squirreltable*."

He sat down on what he supposed she'd call a Squirrelchair.

"Now," she said, "take a good look at the Squirrelboard."

He sighed, but read the newspaper stories that she'd pinned to the noticeboard.

THIEF TAKES BMX

8 YEAR OLD HAS BIRTHDAY BIKE STOLEN

6th BIKE THEFT IN A WEEK

"So, how can I help?" asked Walter, shrugging.

"With your special powers, of course. With your speed and your powerful tail, you can catch the thief and hold him until the police arrive."

"But, how will I know where to find him?"

"Easy," she said. "We'll set a trap. We'll leave your bike unlocked outside the very row of shops where three of the thefts have taken place. You'll be hiding out of sight, watching and waiting. Then, when someone steals the bike – bam! – you pounce!"

On the table was a large piece of paper, which she now flipped over dramatically. It was a really impressive drawing of a row of shops.

"Nice picture," he said. "Did you do it?"

She nodded.

"I was an artist for a while, in my twenties," she said. "I worked with a very famous gentleman called Salvador Dali. Odd man, tremendous moustache. Anyway, let's concentrate." She poked a wrinkly finger at the picture. "Point A," she started, "is where you leave the bike. Point B is where you hide in a bush. Point C is where I'll be sitting. In a bus shelter."

"But won't the thief see you?"

"Perhaps," she said, "but my knees aren't up to crouching in bushes these days. And, anyway, old ladies are virtually invisible. No one pays attention to us. While you are catching the thief, however, I'll be calling the police."

Walter nodded. It sounded like a good plan.

"What about D?" he said, jabbing a finger at the picture.

"Oh," she said. "That's a toilet, in case I need a wee. At my age, you never want to be too far from a loo."

CHAPTER THREE AND A HALF

Which Is Hardly a Chapter At All, Really

Squirrel Boy had been hiding in the bush for almost two hours, now. Mrs Onions, it turned out, didn't need a wee yet, but he was starting to need a break.

People think that being a superhero is all action, but the truth is that there is an awful lot of waiting around. His bottom was numb from all that sitting and his tail was numb from being sat on. He'd had to sit on it, of course, otherwise it would have been poking very conspicuously out of the top of the bush.

I don't know if you've ever sat in a bush for hours, staring at a bicycle as it leant against the front of a shop. But, believe me, it's not so exciting.

So let's move onto the next chapter, where something much more interesting – utterly astounding, in fact – is about to happen.

CHAPTER FOUR

Squirrel Boy heard something scurrying in the bush, and turned away from the bike for a moment to see what it might be.

He saw to his surprise that it was a squirrel. A small and very frightened squirrel.

So terrified that, when it saw Squirrel Boy, instead of running away, it didn't move at all. Not even a twitch, which is very unusual for a squirrel.

But this wasn't the astounding thing. If you were a squirrel and you stumbled upon a huge squirrel-person many times bigger than you, you'd be pretty shocked, too.

No, the completely incredible thing was that Squirrel Boy realised he could speak Squirrelish. The sounds just came into his head and, when the squirrel answered him, he could understand it as plainly as if they'd both been speaking English.

Of course, if I wrote their conversation down in the original language, it would just sound like a lot of clicks, like this:

Walter: Click-click-click-clickety-click.
Squirrel: Click-click.

So I'm translating it into English for you, as best I can, as follows:

"Don't be scared," said Squirrel Boy.

"Yikes!" exclaimed the squirrel. "You can talk, too! What are you?"

"I'm Squirrel Boy. I'm half-person, half-squirrel."

"Blimey!"

"What's your name, little squirrel?"

Squirrels don't have names in the same

way that people do, so I've come up with the nearest human equivalent.

"I'm Trevor Davies," said the squirrel.

"What are you doing in this bush, Trevor Davies?"

"Hiding, and looking for nuts."

In fact, if you ever ask a squirrel what they're doing, they'll almost certainly give you exactly the same answer. When they're awake, looking for nuts and hiding is pretty much all that they do.

Squirrel Boy took a nut from the packet he was holding and held it out on his palm for Trevor, who inspected it, put it in his mouth, and immediately spat it out.

"Oh, yuck! Bleurgh! What was that?"

"A peanut."

Trevor was pulling a face and trying to get the taste out of his mouth.

"What's the disgusting white stuff on the outside?"

There is no squirrel word for 'salt', and it was much too difficult for Squirrel Boy to describe, so he changed the subject.

"Where do you live, Trevor?" he asked.

"In the park. You?"

"Near the park," said Squirrel Boy.

"In a tree?"

"In a house.

"I've always wondered," said Trevor, "what a house is like; inside, I mean."

"It's like a tree, I suppose, but with lots of rooms: bedrooms and a toilet and..."

"Toilet?"

"It's a place where you – you know –

you can do a wee or a poo."

"Blimey!" Trevor spluttered with astonishment. "You mean you don't just do it on the ground?"

Squirrel Boy shook his head and Trevor the squirrel looked at him like he might be crazy.

"What are you doing here, anyway?" asked the squirrel.

"I'm waiting for someone to steal my..." Squirrel Boy started, before realising there was no squirrel word for 'bike', either. "I'm hiding, too," he said instead, which was true, in a way.

"I'd better be off," said the squirrel. "To find some nuts: ones without disgusting white stuff on them."

"Okay. Good luck, Trevor."

"You too, huge mutant squirrel-person."

"Squirrel Boy."

"Oh, yes. 'Squirrel Boy'. Sorry. See you."

And, with that, Trevor Davies the squirrel scurried off out of the bush, while Squirrel Boy kept on waiting for someone to steal his bike.

CHAPTER FIVE

When it happened, it was so sudden that it caught both Squirrel Boy and Mrs Onions by surprise.

They had both been expecting a single thief to walk up to the bike, look shiftily around to make sure that nobody was watching, and ride quickly off.

What actually happened was this:

A gang of mean-looking boys on bikes whizzed down the road, past Squirrel Boy's bush. There were three bikes but four boys; one of them was perched on the crossbar of the middle bike. All of the boys were much bigger and older than Walter, and they were pedalling very quickly indeed.

When they reached the row of shops, they all skidded to a stop, tyres screeching. The boy leapt from the crossbar of the middle bike, jumped onto Walter's bike and then they all rode off, now with four bikes instead of three.

As Mrs Onions dialled the police on her mobile, Squirrel Boy burst out of the bush and sprinted up the road in pursuit of the thieves.

Even at Squirrel Speed, he struggled to catch up but eventually, panting heavily, he was within shouting distance.

"STOP!" he yelled.

They didn't stop, but they did look over their shoulders. And they were utterly astonished to see who – or what – was chasing them. In fact, just the sight of Squirrel Boy was enough to make one of the thieves wobble; he lost control of his bike and crashed into a lamp post. The bike stopped dead, and the boy was flung off like a jockey whose horse had refused a fence. The boy landed on the pavement and rolled three times before coming to a stop.

But the other three kept on going, pedalling even more furiously than before.

Squirrel Boy strained every muscle to catch up and, when he was finally along-side the third bike, he swished his powerful tail and knocked the boy clean off it. The bike clattered to the floor. The boy flew screaming into a hedge.

Now there were only two but they were hurtling away. Squirrel Boy caught up with the second bike and tried the tail trick again, but this time the rider swerved and dodged. Not knowing what else to do, and at full speed, Squirrel Boy leapt onto the back of the bike and grabbed onto the rider, who weaved this way and that to try to shake him off.

Squirrel Boy held on tight with his squirrel claws.

The thief yelped.

Then Squirrel Boy's tail came over his head and started to tickle the thief until he finally let go of the handlebars, fell off the bike, and rolled spectacularly onto the pavement until he came to a stop next to a bin.

But still the last boy kept going.

"That's my bike!" Squirrel Boy wheezed.

"Get lost, freak!" the boy yelled, red-faced.

Squirrel Boy was tiring rapidly by now, but if there was one thing that he disliked more than anything else in the world (other than broccoli) it was being called a freak.

With his last burst of energy, grunting with effort, he flung himself head first at the boy and, in mid-air, grabbed him with his tail, wrenched him off the bike and – before the bike could crash into a wall – Squirrel Boy somersaulted, leapt onto it and skidded to a halt.

The bike thief lay on his back on the pavement, dazed and blinking up at him in disbelief. Squirrel Boy could see the other three boys strewn along the pavement in the distance, and then he saw the lights of the police car as it came to pick them up, one by one. Squirrel Boy knew when it was time to leave.

CHAPTER SIX

"Walter!"

He'd overslept, exhausted by his efforts of last night and, when he blinked open his eyes, he saw his mum standing over him. He was expecting her to say what she usually did in this situation: "Come on, sleepyhead, hurry up, hop out of bed, you'll be late for school." But instead she said, excitedly:

"Have you heard the news? Squirrel Boy stopped a gang of bike thieves last night!"

His mum was determined to solve the mystery of Squirrel Boy's identity, so she could reveal it exclusively on her blog *All about Animals*. Walter knew she would completely freak out if she discovered it was him. This was one secret he needed to keep.

"I've found a clue," she said, breathlessly. Walter had been feeling groggy, but now he sat up in bed, suddenly very awake. "There's a picture of him on the internet," she continued. "It was taken by someone in a passing car, and you can't see his face clearly, but he's definitely wearing a blue jumper."

Walter tried not to show his relief.

"Is that it?" he said. "Lots of people have blue jumpers, Mum."

"Not this jumper. It's just like yours; the same style exactly." The jumper in question was scrumpled on the floor of his room, and they both stared at it now.

"There are probably hundreds of those jumpers," he said. "Thousands."

She shook her head.

"It's handmade, by Nikki from 'Nice Knits' in town. I'm going to call in later and see how many she's made, and if she remembers who bought them."

Walter didn't know what to say. If Nikki told his mum that she'd only made one of those jumpers, his secret would be out. He sighed. He should have been more careful about what clothes he wore as Squirrel Boy. Maybe Mrs Onions' idea of a superhero costume wasn't so bad after all.

"Now," his mum said, brightly, "come on, sleepyhead, hurry up, hop out of bed, you'll be late for school."

Not far away, that same morning, Auberon Steyn was at his table eating badger stew for breakfast (which is completely disgusting for any meal, by the way, but especially breakfast) and Snarl was under the table, gnawing restlessly on a bone, when they heard the newspaper being pushed through the letterbox.

Snarl leapt up so sharply that he banged his head on the table, making stew spill out of its bowl (which made his owner curse), and then he dashed to the door. Snarl treated the newspaper as if it was a small animal he was hunting. He pounced on it and smothered it, clamped it between his ferocious teeth and then rushed it back to his master.

So, whenever Auberon Steyn received the newspaper from his dog, it was always slightly torn and more-than-slightly-drool-spattered. Usually, he would flick quickly through it, muttering about how depressing the world was.

But not this time.

This time, he stared at the front page, utterly transfixed. He instantly forgot about his breakfast, and instead gazed dreamily at the newspaper.

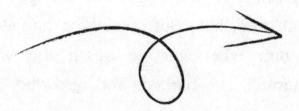

THE TELEGRAPH

BIKE BANDITS BUSTED:

SQUIRREL BOY TRIUMPHS AGAIN!

It was at least a minute before Auberon Steyn could speak.

"How many squirrels have we caught, Snarl?"

Snarl, like most dogs, didn't understand English, except commands like 'sit' and 'walk' and 'kill'. But something happened to him whenever he heard the word 'squirrel': he barked and growled and howled and ground his teeth. In short, he went completely bananas.

"I'll tell you how many we've caught," Auberon Steyn continued. "177. That's how many tails we've got decorating our beautiful home."

He looked around, admiring the limp tails which were nailed to the dank walls all around him.

"But if I can get *that* tail," he added, prodding a stumpy finger at the newspaper, "it would be worth all of those other tails put together. I will go down in history as the greatest squirrel hunter of all time. They'll simply call me: the Squirrel Hunter."

Snarl yelped and growled, but Auberon Steyn was concentrating so deeply on the photo of Squirrel Boy that it was like he was in a trance.

Then, he snapped out of it and wondered just how he could possibly find Squirrel Boy. After all, nobody knew the rodent superhero's real identity, not even the police.

And then a plan came to him, so suddenly that he gasped and dropped his spoon, which clattered to the floor.

He wouldn't need to find Squirrel Boy: instead, he'd do something that would make Squirrel Boy come to him.

Something that would get in the newspaper.

Something horrible.

Something that Squirrel Boy wouldn't be able to ignore.

CHAPTER SEVEN

Saturdays were normally Walter's favourite, because he could do as he pleased. He would usually spend the morning next door with Mrs Onions (and her delicious food) and then sometimes he'd go to the library with his mum or, as a special treat, go to the movies or the zoo. Other times he'd ride his bike to the park, or just lounge around his house reading a book or a comic, or watching TV. That was the thing about Saturdays... there were lots of things that didn't have to be done.

But on this particular Saturday, Walter woke up feeling inexplicably sad.

His mum reported that Nikki from Nice Knits had made ten of those blue jumpers, and couldn't remember who had bought them. This news should have made him happy, but it didn't.

He got dressed, had a piece of toast and brushed his teeth, but he couldn't shake the feeling. Even the thought of a visit next door didn't cheer him up.

"What's up, young man?" Mrs Onions asked him when she opened the door. "You've got a face like a smacked bottom."

Walter shrugged.

"Come in, then, and I'll bring you a slice of my famous egg-and-bacon pie," she said.

"That'll do the trick."

Normally, it would have, but not today. He sat in an armchair, eating a slice of the excellent pie but still feeling blue. Mrs Onions sat in the other chair, drinking tea and staring at him quizzically.

"Is it girl trouble?" she asked, kindly.

He blushed and shook his head. When he was Squirrel Boy, he was pretty confident, but when he was just Walter Kettle, he was still so shy he could hardly talk to girls, let alone have any trouble with them.

"Is it a problem at school?" she asked.

"No."

"At home?"

"I really don't know what it is," he admitted. "I just woke up this morning feeling like this, and I can't seem to snap out of it."

Mrs Onions placed her tea cup carefully on the side table and nodded her head.

"Listen," she said. "All eleven year olds feel like this sometimes. When you're eleven, your body is starting to change into a grown-up's body and your brain is changing, too. But you, Walter, have an even greater challenge than other eleven year olds. You are not only slowly changing into an adult, you are sometimes changing into a squirrel, and very quickly, too. It's no wonder you're feeling a bit confused about everything. Eleven is a difficult age for anyone, let alone a superhero. Mind you," she added, with a chuckle, "I'm seventy-three, and that's a difficult age, too, for different reasons."

"Like what?" he said, relieved to be talking about something other than himself.

"Well, for starters, our bodies don't work so well any more, and our lives don't tend to be as exciting. For another thing, the kind of books that seventy-three year olds read don't usually have lots of pictures in them, and books without pictures aren't nearly as interesting. And, most of all," she added, sadly, "seventy-three year olds don't get to go on bouncy castles."

Walter imagined a bouncy castle full of old people bouncing all over the place, and a smile flickered on his face.

"That's better," Mrs Onions said. "Let's put the TV on and see if we can cheer you up further."

But what they saw on TV only made Walter feel much, much worse.

CHAPTER EIGHT

The newsreader announced, in a sombre voice:

"They are calling it 'The Grange Park Squirrel Massacre'. Joggers and walkers have this morning reported seeing a total of a dozen dead squirrels spread around the park, all of them missing tails. And nobody has any idea who is responsible. There is a hand-written sign, however, nailed to a tree in the park."

The TV screen showed a close-up of the sign:

The report finished, Mrs Onions clicked the news off, and they looked at each other in stunned silence.

When she spoke, she said exactly what Walter had been thinking.

"Do you think," she started, softly, "that the reason you're feeling blue this morning is that you have some kind of squirrel sense? That some part of you knew what had happened to those poor squirrels?"

He nodded. There was another silence.

"Killing squirrels and taking their tails," he muttered in disbelief. "Who would do such a thing?"

"Let's think about it," said Mrs Onions. "Well, for starters, it's almost definitely a man."

"How do you know?"

"When I was in the Secret Service, many years ago, we did a course in handwriting analysis; the chunky letters on that sign are a man's work, I'm pretty certain."

"So that's all we know?"

"And he's not so good at spelling," she added.

He nodded.

"I don't get why he put the sign there," Walter said. "Can't the police just go to the park tonight to arrest him?"

"I'm afraid not. They're very busy. Squirrels aren't pets, you see, and they're not an endangered species. Some people even say they're pests. I'm not sure it's the police's business."

"So he can kill as many squirrels as he wants?"

"Well, no,' she said. "Animal cruelty is a crime. It's just not a police priority, I suppose."

"So, then, I'll have to do something about it," Walter said, standing up and marching to the spare room (better known as Squirrel Boy Headquarters). He came back five minutes later waving a piece of paper he'd scribbled a picture on.

"What's that?" she asked. "Modern art?"

"It's my plan," he said, proudly.

"That's your plan?" she said.

"I'll sneak out of my bedroom window at night, go to the park, and wait for him to come."

She frowned.

"Let me get this straight: you're a ten-year-old boy, and your plan is to go to a park and jump out at a man who not only enjoys killing things, but also seems to have a very good aim."

"But I won't be a normal boy," Walter explained. "I'll be Squirrel Boy."

Mrs Onions shook her head.

"So your plan is for you – in the form of a giant squirrel – to jump out at a man who enjoys killing squirrels?"

He nodded. She sighed.

"Do you see that picture up there?" she asked, pointing out a photo. She was standing next to a man, and both of them were wearing chef's hats. "That's Hedley Zest, the famous chef. I worked with him for a while. That egg-and-bacon pie recipe is his. And not many people know this, but he is also the inventor of Sausage-Flavoured Ice Cream. Have you ever tasted sausage-flavour ice cream?"

"No," said Walter.

"Well," she went on, "there is a very good reason for that. It's absolutely terrible. Disgusting. Horrible. And this idea of yours," she added, "is even worse than that."

But Walter had made up his mind and

there was nothing that Mrs Onions could say that would talk him out of it.

CHAPTER NINE

When he got home, his mum was in a tizz and making a placard.

"I thought it was tigers you were saving this week," Walter said.

"Did you hear the news?" she said, passionately. "Squirrels are being killed, right here in our local park. Poor little creatures. And I'm going to do something about it."

"By making a sign?"

"By going to the park tonight

and protesting.

He stared at her.

"Please don't, Mum. It might be really dangerous."

"It won't just be me. Some of the others will be going, too."

His mum worked for Friends of the Animals; a charity. He'd met some of the people. They all seemed to be kind and peaceful people; much too nice to stop a crazy squirrel-killing maniac.

"Please don't go, Mum," Walter begged. She looked at him seriously for a few moments.

"Okay," she said, eventually.

Walter was surprised, because usually his mum was just like him: when she made up her mind to do something, she couldn't be talked out of it; like the time she wore rainbow leggings and a lime-green poncho to take him to school. But now she just got on with painting the placard.

"There's only one 'R' in squirrel, right?"

Walter shook his head.

"If you're not going," he said, "why are you still doing the sign?"

"One of the others might take it with them," she said, and then, pausing the paintbrush mid-stroke, she looked at him seriously. "Is everything okay with you, Walter?"

"Yes," he said.

"It's just that you don't seem like your normal self today. Is something wrong at school?"

He shook his head.

"Girl trouble?" she asked.

He sighed. Why did everyone think he was having girl problems?

"Because," she went on, regardless, "you know you can talk to me, don't you? I was a girl once. Maybe I can help."

He blushed. He really did have the most embarrassing mum in the history of the world.

"It's not girls, Mum."

"So, what is it? Something's the matter. Mums know these things. It's like an extra sense."

When his mum mentioned the extra sense, it made him want to tell her everything. Keeping secrets was awful, especially from his mum. *I turn into a squirrel sometimes.* That's what he wanted to say. But he knew his mum would completely lose the plot, so instead he said:

"I'm okay, Mum. Honest."

And then he went to his room to go over his plan for that night.

The more he thought about it, the more nervous he became.

CHAPTER MINUS FORTY-SEVEN

When Auberon Steyn was ten years old – which was a very, very long time ago – his parents took him to a petting zoo.

He didn't hate animals, not yet, but he was the type of rough, thoughtless boy who couldn't be gentle with anything. Toys didn't last very long in the Steyn household. He had more teddy bears without heads than with them.

So, on his visit to the petting zoo, when his mum and dad's backs were turned,

Auberon squeezed a squirming rabbit too hard, pulled on a piglet's corkscrew tail and threw a chick to see if it could fly. It couldn't. Then he tugged the chin hair of a goat and pulled the wool of a lamb to see if it would come off. It didn't.

Rabbits and pigs and sheep, and so on, can't talk to each other, of course. They don't speak the same language. Sheep speak 'baa', pigs speak 'oink' and rabbits don't say much of anything. But something miraculous happened in the petting zoo that day: all the animals, all at the same moment, decided that they'd had enough.

Auberon Steyn didn't know what had hit him.

In fact, several things hit him.

The goat was first. It sneaked up behind him, took a run-up and – at full pelt – butted Auberon's bottom: a butt-butt. This knocked the boy flat on his face, into the dirt.

He yelped, but it was muffled by the dirt and so didn't get his mum and dad's attention. And, for Auberon Steyn, the ordeal was only just beginning:

A pig – and by no means a small pig – jumped onto his back. A chicken pecked at his forehead. The lamb kicked him in the side. The rabbit, of course, couldn't do much, but was nevertheless enjoying the show.

Finally, a nearby squirrel, who had been watching on, climbed the fence into the petting zoo, bounded over and sank its teeth into Auberon's plump bottom.

"Yeeeooowww!"

This time his parents spun around to see their only son under a pile of angry young animals, squealing for help.

The Steyns never went back to the petting zoo and never spoke of the incident, but Auberon would never forget. It was the day his hatred for animals began.

He spent several years teasing local cats. And when his dad bought him a catapult for his fifteenth birthday, he took up hunting.

It was squirrels that he hated the most. He'd done nothing to that squirrel, but it had climbed on top of him and chomped his poor defenceless bottom. Squirrels. There was something about their twitchy little faces and their sneaky way of getting around that Auberon Steyn loathed.

One evening, a few years ago now, when he was hunting squirrels in the park, a stray dog bounded over. The dog looked mean and seemed to hate squirrels as much as Auberon Steyn did. So he took the dog home, and called it Snarl.

This evening, Auberon Steyn sat in his dank house, giddy with excitement. He felt like a child on Christmas morning, about to get the best present of his life. Auberon Steyn was about to collect a squirrel tail.

And not just any tail: it would be the tail of the biggest squirrel the world had ever seen.

CHAPTER TEN

Walter lay in bed, pretending to be asleep. After his mum came in to kiss him goodnight, he waited five more minutes and then, lying there in the dark, ate a peanut.

When he felt the familiar tingling, he wriggled carefully out of bed.

There was the burning sensation as his tail shot out.

Then his hands and feet throbbed, and out came the claws.

Now his cheeks puffed out, and the

change was complete.

He quietly stuffed a pillow and some clothes under his duvet, so even if his mum peeked into his room, it would look like he was in bed.

He put on a plain black T-shirt and dark pyjama bottoms – he'd learned his lesson after the blue jumper thing – and finally put on his yellow mask. Then, very quietly, he opened his bedroom window and edged outside.

Climbing down the side of the house wasn't a big deal. Walter was usually terrified of heights, but when he was Squirrel Boy things like this didn't worry him. He scampered down in seconds, his claws digging into the spaces between the bricks as he did.

Once he was on the ground, he bounded to the park in the moonlight.

He hadn't realised before, but his night-vision improved when he was Squirrel Boy, too. The park was dark but he could clearly make out trees and the few nocturnal animals that came out: a fox, a hedgehog, but no squirrels, and no people.

He found a thick tree to hide behind and waited, but the longer he waited, the more nervous he got. Even the smallest noise – an animal scurrying, the snap of a twig – made him jumpy.

When he finally saw the man approaching, Squirrel Boy's heart was thumping in his chest, but it wasn't really the man that scared him: he was small and round and waddled when he walked.

No, the truly terrifying thing was beside
the man. A dog. A big, angry-looking dog,
straining at the leash.

Usually, Walter wasn't particularly afraid of dogs. But, as Squirrel Boy, something strange was happening: it was like his entire body was begging him to run away. The squirrel part of him was absolutely petrified.

He had come to the park to confront the man but now all he wanted to do was get as far away as possible.

The man had a torch in one hand and what looked like a small stick in the other. He was shining the torch around, sweeping the beam of light across the park.

The dog was barking urgently.

Squirrel Boy needed to make a decision. He could run quickly, he knew, but dogs were fast, too. Would he be able to outrun the dog? He couldn't be sure.

The barking of the dog was getting closer and more agitated, and Walter was getting tenser and tenser.

"What is it, Snarl?" the man was shouting. "Squirrels?"

This made the dog even crazier.

"Go get him, boy!" the man said as he released the dog. Snarl burst away and raced straight towards Squirrel Boy's tree.

Squirrel Boy could hardly breathe. He glanced up into the branches of the tree that he was hiding behind and scrambled up until he was out of reach and partly hidden by branches.

The dog skidded to a stop at the base of the tree and kept on barking and jumping up until the man eventually caught up.

Auberon Steyn yanked the dog's collar

to quieten him and soon there was an eerie silence again – just the rustling of the leaves, the wheezing of the man, and the panting of the dog. Squirrel Boy could hear his own breathing, too: short and fast and shallow.

Then the man shone the torch into the branches, cleared his throat and yelled:

"I know you're up there, Squirrel Boy!"

Squirrel Boy jolted in shock at the sound of his name.

"Snarl here never mistakes the smell of a squirrel," the man went on. "And for him to be barking like that, it must be a very big squirrel indeed."

The dog started barking crazily again and Auberon Steyn grabbed his collar to shush him.

"I set a trap for you, Squirrel Boy," the man boasted, "and you hopped right into it. I knew you'd come when you heard about those other squirrels. But squirrels are vermin. And you, Squirrel Boy, are the biggest pest of all."

Through the branches, Walter saw with horror what was in the man's other hand. It wasn't a small stick. It was a catapult.

And then the torch beam shone into his eyes and blinded him for a moment.

"Aha," said Auberon Steyn, chuckling to himself. "There you are. Gotcha. And what a fine tail, if I may say so."

Squirrel Boy couldn't see what the man was doing. The light from the torch dazzled him and even squinting didn't help.

"I only want your tail, that's all," said the

Squirrel Hunter, calmly. "The rest of you I have no use for. Now, we can do this two ways. You can either come down by yourself or..." he grinned horribly,"...I can use my catapult to get you down. And I'm a very, very accurate shot."

When Squirrel Boy didn't respond, the man chuckled again and said: "Okay, have it your way. To be honest, this way is much more fun."

With that, he placed a rock the size of a plum into the catapult and took aim into the branches of the tree. Squirrel Boy shuffled further down the branch, and the rock whistled past his shoulder. His tail was usually an effective shield, but would be no match for a rock going at that speed, which he couldn't even see.

So he decided to climb to the top of the tree, further away, before the next shot. He moved quickly, but the branches higher up were thinner and weaker: only strong enough to hold birds and regular-sized squirrels.

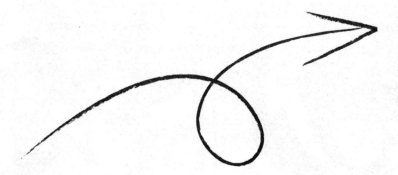

CRACK!

AAAARRGGHH!

THUD!

WOOFWOOFWOOFWOOF!

CHAPTER TWELVE

The crack was the sound of the branch snapping.

The aaaaarrggghhh was the noise that came out of Squirrel Boy's mouth as he plummeted.

The thud was him hitting the ground.

The next sound, other than Snarl's constant barking, was Auberon Steyn's horrible, gurgly voice as he leant over Squirrel Boy's motionless body.

"He's unconscious. Perfect. Perfect. I'll hack his tail off and leave him here." He pulled a hunting knife from the sheath dangling at his hip. The blade glinted horribly in the moonlight. He patted Snarl triumphantly. "What a tail! So plush. I fancy that I'll use it as a pillow, to remind me, as I fall asleep each night, that I am the greatest, the most incredible squirrel hunter of..."

THWACK!

The thwack was the sound of a big wooden sign smacking into the Squirrel Hunter's head. The sign said:

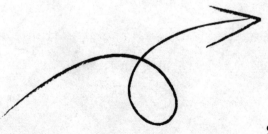

CHAPTER THIRTEEN

Walter's mum had sneaked out of the house ten minutes after her son.

She'd been planning to keep her promise to Walter, but then she'd thought about those poor animals and realised that she couldn't sit around at home while someone might be killing squirrels.

Besides, she thought, Walter was fast asleep and would never know she'd been gone.

She met two other members of Friends

of the Animals at the entrance of the park, and all three of them had signs. There was a sweet younger woman called Sarah, with glasses and very long hair, and a sign which said 'Leave Wildlife Alone'. Next to her was a little old lady called Iris whose sign said 'No To Cruelty'.

They'd spotted the beam from the man's torch, heard the dog, and crept over to him, from behind. When the heavy thing – whatever it was – had fallen from the tree, they'd hurried over, and the barking of the dog meant that the man didn't hear them coming.

Walter's mum was the first to reach him, and what happened next happened in an instant. She saw the Squirrel Hunter's face and recognised him as the horrible man who'd been so rude about the tiger petition. Then she noticed the knife in his hand. And then she saw the thing that was lying helpless on the ground was none other than Squirrel Boy.

Angela Kettle didn't believe in violence. She had been planning to confront the person who was killing all the squirrels and talk to him about the error of his ways. So what she did next was astonishing, even to her. She instinctively swung the sign like it was an enormous fly swat and, using all her strength, thwacked it into the back of Auberon Steyn's head.

He yelped and stumbled and dropped the knife. To stop him from picking it up, the other two women joined in by hitting him with their signs.

When Squirrel Boy blinked open his eyes, he thought he was dreaming.

His mum and two of her friends were surrounding the Squirrel Hunter, who was cursing at them:

"Stop it, you lunatics! Stop hitting me! Squirrels are pests! All animals are pests!"

Iris, the little old lady with the 'No To Cruelty' sign, whacked him on the head with it.

"Ow!" he yelped, and then Sarah joined in again with her 'Leave Wildlife Alone' sign, smacking him very hard on the bottom with it.

"Leave wildlife alone?" he read, as she swung back the sign to hit him again. "Leave me alone, more like!"

"Only if you promise to stop killing

squirrels," said Angela Kettle.

"Never!" he said. "Get them, Snarl!"

But Snarl wasn't the cleverest dog in the world. His brain was much smaller than his bite. He didn't know whether to protect his master, attack the women, or pounce on Squirrel Boy, so he ended up running around, chasing his tail, barking ferociously.

Auberon Steyn backed away very quickly and, eventually, the dog followed him.

While this was happening, Squirrel Boy picked himself up carefully and, when he was sure that no bones were broken and the women were safe, he picked up the knife and catapult from the ground and ran off towards home, in the opposite direction from Auberon Steyn. He tossed the weapons into the nearest bin, kept on running and didn't look back till he was most of the way home.

When he got there, he climbed the wall of his house and slipped in through his bedroom window.

Then he lay in bed, his heart beating fast, wondering if his mum had recognised him. He didn't think so: it had been dark; he'd been wearing a mask; and she'd been preoccupied with the Squirrel Hunter. But he couldn't be sure.

After a few minutes, his heartbeat slowed down and his tired body changed back into human form. Then he heard his mum coming back into the house and tiptoeing upstairs. When she checked on him, he pretended to be asleep. And then, seconds later, completely exhausted, he drifted off to sleep for real.

CHAPTER FOURTEEN

The Kettles both got up late the next morning.

Walter lay in bed for a long time, feeling sore from the fall and worn-out from all the drama of last night.

He'd been very lucky, he knew. If his mum and her friends hadn't been there, who knows what would have happened? And what kind of superhero, he wondered, did that make him? Other superheroes got help all the time, from each other, but to his knowledge no other superheroes ever got help from their mums.

It was much later than usual when Walter and his mum had breakfast together, and they were both looking uncomfortable. Neither of them could look at the other, so they both concentrated on their bran flakes.

And then Angela Kettle put down her spoon and stared at her son.

"Walter," she started, "being honest is very important, you know."

He nodded, his face feeling hot. Did she know? Had she recognised him last night? He opened his mouth to confess, but then she continued:

"I haven't been honest with you, Walter, and that's a terrible example for a mum to set. Last night, you see, I went to the park."

Walter wasn't much of an actor but he tried to look incredibly surprised.

"I know I said I wouldn't go," she continued, "and I feel awful for being dishonest, but I'm actually glad I went. We stopped the man who'd been hunting those squirrels and, it's hard to believe, but we also saved Squirrel Boy."

Walter didn't say anything.

"I recognised him," she added, and Walter almost choked on his bran flakes.

"You recognised Squirrel Boy?" he said, weakly.

"No," she said, and he silently sighed with relief. "It all happened so quickly. By the time we'd frightened off that horrible man, Squirrel Boy had run off. I'm absolutely kicking myself. It was a golden chance to talk to him. No, I mean I recognised the man who'd been killing those squirrels. I'd knocked on his door when I was doing the tiger petition last week. He was incredibly rude. I don't know his name, but I do know his address: 41, Gattling Street. I've got half a mind to go there and have words with him."

"No, Mum! Please don't go!"

She looked at him for a few seconds.

"OK," she said, eventually.

"Promise?"

"I promise. Animals are very important to me, but you, Walter, are by far the most precious thing in my world."

She got up and gave him a hug, before sitting back down.

"But I'm writing a blog about last night,

and then I'm going to find out the Squirrel Hunter's name and expose him as the cruel man that he is. Now," she continued, "was there something that you wanted to say?"

Walter shook his head.

CHAPTER FIFTEEN

Only one week later, before his mum had even discovered the Squirrel Hunter's real name, Walter woke up feeling sad again.

It was a clear, sunny Saturday morning, and it seemed that there was nothing at all to be unhappy about. His mum would be going out with some friends that evening, which meant that Walter would be having a sleepover at Mrs Onions' place. He always looked forward to that: he'd get to stay up late, eat delicious food, and they both loved watching action movies. Plus, with Mrs Onions, he could talk about Squirrel Boy things, or listen to another exciting instalment in her incredible life. It was never boring.

But instead he woke up feeling miserable. He immediately wondered, of course, if it was his squirrel sense again, telling him that something was wrong. And so, without eating breakfast, he raced his bike to the park to investigate.

The park looked peaceful enough and there were no dead squirrels around, but something didn't feel right. It felt too quiet, somehow.

He propped his bike against a tree (it was safer to leave bikes these days, thanks to him), and then he popped a peanut in his mouth and waited.

When the transformation happened, he put on his mask and started climbing the tree. He looked in all the nooks in the trunk, every squirrel-sized hiding place, but no squirrels were around, just a couple of startled birds that flew off as soon as they saw him.

He started talking in Squirrelish as he searched: a series of rapid-fire clicks that meant 'Is anyone there?', but there was no response.

Careful to stay out of sight of any people in the park – joggers or walkers – he climbed back down, scampered to the next tree, and raced up it.

And then another. And another, getting more desperate all the time. The squirrels were all either hiding or, he thought, miserably, they were all dead.

It was in the fifth tree that something happened.

He climbed stealthily to the top, clicking the same question over and over, until eventually an answer came: a soft clicking, almost a whisper.

"Squirrel Boy?" came the voice. "Is that you?"

Just a nose and whiskers were poking out of a crevice in the tree.

Now, all squirrels might look alike to you or me but, then, we're not half-squirrel – at least, I certainly hope you're not. When he saw the nose and whiskers, Squirrel Boy knew immediately that it was Trevor.

"Am I glad to see you!" Squirrel Boy

gushed. "Where's everyone else?"

"Hiding," he said. "They came again last night... the man and the dog. Everyone's terrified! And so would you be if you'd seen them."

"I have seen them. And, what's more, I know where they live."

"Yikes!" said Trevor. "Tell me where and I'll keep well clear of it."

"Actually," Squirrel Boy said, "I was thinking of paying him a visit. Tonight!"

"Have you completely lost your mind?" spluttered Trevor, his whole head now poking out of the hole.

"And I'd like to take you with me," Squirrel Boy added.

"What?" said Trevor. (Squirrels don't have polite phrases like 'excuse me?' or 'pardon?', like we do.) "You want me to visit the home of a squirrel-murderer?"

"Not just me and you," said Squirrel Boy breathlessly. "I want to take all the squirrels we can find."

"You have lost your mind," Trevor mumbled.

"Maybe," said Squirrel Boy. "But, if we don't do something fast, that horrible man will keep coming and coming and coming until there are no more squirrels left. He'll kill every last one of us."

CHAPTER SIXTEEN

Later that afternoon, in a haze of smoke in Mrs Onions' front room, Walter explained his plan to her. She was listening carefully and puffing away on her pipe.

She waited for him to finish before putting the pipe down and, with an amused look in her eyes, slowly shook her head.

"That," she said, firmly, "is absolutely your most stupid plan yet. Even worse than the last one. And that last plan, remember, almost got you killed."

"But nothing else will work," Walter persisted. "Even being bashed by women with signs didn't stop him. We need to do something so incredible that it will shock him into changing his ways. And, anyway, didn't you do any crazy things when you were younger?"

A glance around the room at some of the framed photographs was all Mrs Onions needed to remind herself.

"It's extremely dangerous," she said eventually. "And it might backfire spectacularly." She took a deep breath. "But," she added, "if you feel like you have to..."

"And I need to do it tonight," he added, "so my mum won't realise that I've gone."

She picked up her pipe and puffed on it

for a very long time, thinking.

"There is one small adjustment I need to make to the plan," she said.

"Okay," he said. "What is it?"

"I will be coming along," she announced.

"No way," he said. "It's much too dangerous."

She chuckled.

"I've flown a fighter plane under enemy fire," she said, pointing at a small, faded photo hanging on the wall where she was wearing an old-fashioned pilot's helmet and goggles. "I've swum with sharks, and not cute little baby sharks, either. Big grown-up sharks, with teeth like knives. I've even eaten broccoli and lived to tell the tale."

"But you're... well, you're..."

"Old?"

"I was going to say 'not so young any more'," he explained.

"Cheeky imp," she said, grinning. "Let me tell you something, young man. When you went to the park the other night, all by yourself, and walked straight into that horrible man's trap – that was my fault. I should have realised. If anything had happened to you, I would never have forgiven myself. And tonight I'm supposed to be looking after you: your mum is trusting me to be responsible."

"But..."

"And, anyway, other superheroes have sidekicks," she continued. "Batman, for example, has Robin."

"But Robin," Walter said, "isn't a seventy-three-year-old lady with dodgy knees."

But she just smiled back at him, her eyes twinkling, and he knew that he wouldn't be able to change her mind.

"You'll need a disguise," Walter muttered, "so he won't recognise you."

"I've already thought about that," she said, and hobbled off to her bedroom.

When she came back into the front room ten minutes later, his eyebrows shot up and his mouth dropped open.

"What do you think?" she said, swishing the cape.

After a while, he managed to say:

"What are you supposed to be? Spider Pensioner?"

"I'm calling myself the Black Widow," she announced. "A widow, obviously, because my husband died. Black, because I had a lot of material left over from a dress I once made. And 'black widow' is also the name of a deadly spider."

"But you don't have any spider powers," Walter pointed out, "like shooting webs or swinging between buildings."

"Well," she said, "spiders are very patient creatures, and so am I."

"'Patience' isn't really a superpower," said Walter.

"True. But I was a spy in my younger days, and I still have a couple of tricks up my sleeve. Plus, I'm good at other useful things, like baking and tying knots."

Walter sighed. Those things, he thought, might be very useful in the Girl Guides, but not for a superhero's sidekick.

But he was wrong. Those talents came in very handy, very soon indeed.

CHAPTER SEVENTEEN

Mrs Onions hadn't only made herself a costume – she'd made one for Walter, too After the blue jumper thing, he had to be more careful. She laid it out on the table in Squirrel Boy HQ and he tried it on. It fitted nicely and, when he checked it in the mirror, he had to admit, it looked kind of cool.

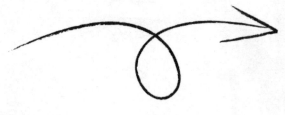

Mrs Onions made a glass of milk for Walter and a cup of tea for herself, still wearing the Black Widow outfit, minus the mask. Walter wondered out loud where she'd put it, and she patted the black pouch at her hip.

"What else is in there?" he asked.

"Some things that might come in very handy on our mission," she said, unzipping the pouch and pulling out what looked like a packet of mints.

Walter had watched enough spy movies to guess that the 'packet of mints' was really an incredible gadget in disguise.

"Let me guess," he said, staring at the packet. "It's actually a stun gun, or a spy camera."

"No," she said, looking at him curiously.

"It's a packet of mints. The word 'mints' on the side is a clue."

"Why are you taking some mints?"

"You never know when you'll need fresh breath, Walter. You also never know when you'll need a handkerchief," she said, pulling one out of the pouch. And I've also got this."

She slowly pulled out a four-metre length of rope hand over hand, like she was a magician pulling a link of scarves out of a top hat.

"I know a knot that will do just the trick for our plan," she said, and held up the ends of the rope to demonstrate. "I learnt it in my sailing days. It's the knot that pirates tied people up with. First, you put the left over the right, and under, then loop it around, like this, then turn it, twist it through, do a figure of eight, loop it backwards, do a final tuck and, hey presto, there's your knot. It's quite simple, really," she said.

Walter frowned. Maybe it was a good idea that she'd be coming with him, after all.

Then it was time to work on the dog biscuit. She used the basic recipe from her delicious cookies, but instead of sugar (which dogs don't like), she sprinkled in half a sleeping tablet. She moulded it into the shape of a bone (so it looked like a dog treat), baked it in the oven and then left it out to cool.

The light outside had faded and Walter's tummy started to feel all light and wobbly as he thought about all the things that could go wrong. For the plan to work, the Squirrel Hunter would have to be at home, asleep in bed, and Walter would have to sneak into the house. Also, some squirrels would need to turn up on time.

Squirrels don't have clocks, of course. If you were to say "I'll meet you at a quarter past eight" to a squirrel, it would look blankly back at you. So, Walter had told Trevor only that he'd turn up when it was dark, at that same tree. But he had no idea if any other squirrels would be there.

CHAPTER EIGHTEEN

When Squirrel Boy arrived at the park, it was dark and eerily quiet. He was alone. Mrs Onions would be meeting him outside the Squirrel Hunter's house.

He approached the tree, out of breath, but no squirrels were around. He clicked Trevor's name, but nothing happened, and his shoulders slumped as he figured that he'd have to carry out the entire plan with only a seventy-three-year-old woman for help.

But then the leaves rustled and suddenly there was Trevor, racing down the tree, followed by another squirrel, then another, and then two more, and suddenly there was a flood of brown as squirrel after squirrel scampered down the trunk.

Soon there were forty or fifty squirrels at Squirrel Boy's feet.

"Everyone," clicked Trevor, loudly, silencing the other squirrels, "this is Squirrel Boy. Squirrel Boy, this is Bob Stevens, Sally Godden, Matthew Wood and his brother Hamish, Alice Black, Oscar..."

"Hello, everyone," Squirrel Boy interrupted, worried that it would be morning before all the introductions were completed, and he didn't want to be late for Mrs Onions, who was on her way to the house. Then, to Trevor, he said:

"I didn't know there were this many squirrels in the park."

"There aren't," said Trevor. "Not since that terrible man came along. You're looking at pretty much all the squirrels that are left in the whole town. They just wanted to help. So, what's the plan?"

Squirrel Boy explained everything, and the squirrels listened in stunned silence. He was worried they would change their minds when they heard the plan but, when he set off, the army of squirrels dutifully followed him: down back streets and unlit paths, so they wouldn't be seen. The sight of a giant squirrel leading a huge pack of smaller squirrels would no doubt have attracted attention, and he didn't want attention.

As they were bounding down an alley like a wave of brown, Squirrel Boy started to have second thoughts. Maybe Mrs Onions had been right the first time: perhaps it was the stupidest plan in the history of stupid plans. Perhaps it was even worse than sausage ice cream. But they were already approaching the house, and it was too late to back out now.

When they arrived at Auberon Steyn's house, Mrs Onions was waiting, in costume. They all sneaked in through the gate and hid in the overgrown grass and weeds of the front garden.

Squirrel Boy could smell that the dog was home, and saw that all the lights were off in the house, which meant that the Squirrel Hunter was almost certainly in bed.

It would only be a matter of time before Snarl picked up the scent of so many squirrels, so Squirrel Boy knew he had to act quickly. If the dog started barking, the Squirrel Hunter would wake up, and the plan would be completely ruined.

So Squirrel Boy sprinted to the front door, took the dog biscuit from his pocket and pushed it through the letter box. The dog snaffled it up immediately and, only seconds later, there was the soft thud of him hitting the floor unconscious. And then there was no sound at all, other than the nervous clicking of the squirrels as they whispered to each other in the garden.

"Okay," clicked Squirrel Boy. "It's time."

CHAPTER NINETEEN

Squirrel Boy started to scale the side wall of the house. It was mossy and slippy, and twice he lost his footing, but he clung on and managed to pull himself up to the small bathroom window. Earlier that day, while on surveillance, he'd seen it was open a tiny bit.

The window was not much bigger than a shoebox. It was stiff, too, but eventually he forced it open wider and then peered inside the bathroom to check it was empty.

It was. He squeezed in, was stuck for a panicky moment, wriggled and then dropped softly onto the carpet. The light was off but with his squirrel vision he could see a toilet, a shower with a torn curtain, and a sink. On the sink was one toothbrush, a small cake of soap and a shaving brush made out of badger hair.

Squirrel Boy eased the bathroom door open and tentatively poked his head out. He saw with great relief that the Squirrel Hunter's bedroom door was closed.

Squirrel Boy edged out of the bathroom and, very slowly, very careful not to make the tiniest noise, tiptoed downstairs.

At the bottom, when he saw the sleeping dog right up against the door, his whole body tensed up, terrified. He couldn't move. But then he took a deep breath and knew what he had to do: he walked up to the dog, crouched and, straining, managed to move it a few centimetres so he could open the door just enough.

Mrs Onions squeezed into the house, followed one at a time by all the squirrels.

When each one saw Snarl, they froze for a moment, just like Squirrel Boy had done, but then, one by one, they bravely skirted around the dog and, very quietly, followed Squirrel Boy and the Black Widow upstairs.

Knowing that one sudden noise might wake up the Squirrel Hunter, Squirrel Boy trod lightly and led Mrs Onions by the hand in the dark so that she wouldn't bump into anything.

He hesitated outside the bedroom, and wondered how it had come to this: here he was, in a stranger's house late at night, about to walk into his bedroom, followed by an old lady and forty or fifty squirrels.

Then, very carefully, he pushed open the door, a centimetre at a time, until he could peer through the opening.

The man was sprawled on the bed, belly up, snoring, his hands either side of his head on the pillow.

Squirrel Boy stepped into the room first, as softly as he could. The Black Widow next. Then, very nervously, all the squirrels.

CHAPTER TWENTY

The Black Widow carefully took out the length of rope from her pouch. Next, Trevor the squirrel shuffled over to her, clenched one end of the rope between his teeth and, very slowly and very, very gently, hopped onto the bed and trailed the rope over the Squirrel Hunter's portly tummy. Squirrel Boy could hardly breathe: this was the part of the plan that could go very badly wrong. One misplaced paw from Trevor, the man would wake up and then there would be chaos.

They didn't want him to wake up. Not yet.

Trevor moved across the tummy as lightly as he could, like he was climbing a small hill: a hill that wobbled slightly with every breath that the Squirrel Hunter took. Trevor got to the top of the hill and stepped down the other side, arrived at the edge of the bed, hopped down to the floor and dragged the rope back under the bed.

When he scurried back out, Mrs Onions, very nimbly, tied a knot in the middle and handed the end of the rope back to Trevor, who scurried off towards the pillow.

Very carefully indeed, he looped the rope around the Squirrel Hunter's wrists and around the headboard. Mrs Onions tiptoed forward and tied an elaborate knot.

It needed to be very tight, she knew. She yanked on the rope as she finished, and the pressure on the Squirrel Hunter's wrists was enough to wake him up. This was okay. Now that he was tied up, they wanted him awake.

He groaned and opened his eyes groggily, but his eyes didn't adjust to the dark straight away, and he couldn't see anything.

He wriggled – or, at least, he tried to. When he realised he couldn't move, he groped for the bedside lamp. That's when he found that his hands couldn't move either. And now he really started to panic. He moaned loudly from fear and confusion, and tried to wriggle again.

Squirrel Boy clicked on the bedside lamp.

What Auberon Steyn saw stopped him mid-breath. His eyes were wide and his mouth, too, gaped open, but all that came out of it was the tiniest of squeaks.

He glanced feverishly around the room and saw, in this order: Squirrel Boy, an old lady dressed in a black costume, and a huge number of squirrels. In his bedroom.

Unable to pinch himself, he blinked several times to wake himself up from this nightmare, and then shook his head violently, but this didn't work, either.

"Sorry," said Squirrel Boy, "but this is no dream."

"Snarl!" yelled Auberon Steyn ferociously, spraying flecks of spittle as he did. "Snarl! Come here! Kill!"

Squirrel Boy shook his head.

"Your dog's having a nap, I'm afraid," he said. "Don't worry. He'll wake up in the morning."

Auberon Steyn tried one more time to writhe free of the rope, but it was no use.

For the first time, Squirrel Boy noticed the many squirrel tails that were nailed to the wall. The squirrels had seen them, too, and were twitching and clicking angrily to each other.

Trevor was staring at the tail which was nailed to the wall directly behind Auberon Steyn's head.

"That's Brian Jackson's tail," Trevor muttered, sadly. "Alas, poor Brian. I knew him well."

Squirrel Boy spoke to the man.

"We came to tell you to stop killing squirrels."

"Never!" he spluttered. He was kicking his legs and writhing, but that only made the knot tighter. His face was deep red with anger. "Vermin! Pests! Nut-eating idiots! Get out of my room!"

Squirrel Boy clicked a message to the squirrels.

They knew what to do.

CHAPTER TWENTY-ONE

The squirrels – all forty-seven of them – quickly climbed onto the bed and, before Auberon Steyn knew it, they had completely covered his arms and tummy like they were some kind of very heavy rodenty jumper, leaving only his wobbling head and thrashing legs squirrel-free. When he realised – very quickly – that he was completely trapped, he stopped struggling altogether. His round face had changed from red to purplish with rage, but all of a sudden it was pale from utter terror. It made him remember the time at the petting zoo, and he started whimpering.

You might think that having almost fifty squirrels on top of you would be pretty uncomfortable, but not too painful. But you'd be very wrong. Squirrels are very big fidgets indeed. And with every movement of every squirrel on his body, their pointy claws jabbed him like he was a huge pincushion, and their tails tickled him. It was absolute torture.

"Get! Them! Off! Me!" he yelled.

Squirrel Boy leaned in close to Auberon Steyn.

"They'll get off," he said softly, "if you promise to leave them alone. If so much as one more squirrel gets harmed, we'll be back to get revenge. And next time, we won't be so friendly."

The Squirrel Hunter was quiet for a few seconds and then, very slightly, nodded.

"Okay," he said, weakly.

"Do you promise to leave them alone?"

"Yes," he squeaked, in a tiny voice.

"All animals?"

He nodded.

Squirrel Boy immediately clicked the message to the squirrels, and so they clambered off the bed, jabbing Auberon Steyn deliberately as they went.

He yelped, and then he stared angrily at Mrs Onions.

"And what in hell's name are you doing here, you old biddy?" he spluttered, squinting at the BW on her costume. "What are you?" he sneered. "Batty Witch? Bonkers Woman?"

"Close," she said, coolly. "I'm Black Widow."

"No," he said, fiercely. "You're just an old woman in a very stupid costume."

Without taking her eyes off him, she calmly delved into her pouch and took out her white handkerchief.

"See?" he said, incandescent with rage. "Whoever heard of a superhero with a hanky? You're an embarrassment. You're pathetic."

She stepped towards the bed, careful not to tread on a squirrel, leaned towards him and quickly placed the hanky over his mouth and nose. Immediately, he fell asleep.

Squirrel Boy looked at her in amazement.

"Chloroform," she said. "It knocks you out. I still had a small bottle left over from my spy days, and I sprayed it onto the hanky earlier. He'll only sleep for a few minutes, but it should be enough time for us to untie him and get out of here."

She undid the knots and then stuffed the rope and the handkerchief back into her pouch. With the man still unconscious, Squirrel Boy, the Black Widow and the squirrels went downstairs past the sleeping dog and out of the front door, into the overgrown garden.

On the way out, Walter spotted an envelope on a shelf, with the Squirrel Hunter's address and the name Auberon Steyn. He'd remember that and tell his mum for her blog. He'd say that he found out the name from someone at school.

In the garden, Trevor approached Squirrel Boy.

"Thanks," he clicked. "For everything. You know where to find me if you ever need help."

Squirrel Boy nodded and, as the pack of squirrels bounded off down the road, happily back to their trees, he and Mrs Onions walked home at a much slower pace. They'd taken off their masks, he'd tucked in his tail, and it was dark, so unless you were looking very carefully, you would have taken them for an old lady walking with her grandson.

"Squirrel Boy and the Black Widow!" she said, chuckling to herself. "An amazing team!"

Then she felt a sneeze coming on, pulled out the hankie and went to blow her nose.

This was a big mistake, of course.

She was unconscious before she'd even had a chance to blow. Squirrel Boy caught her as she was falling, and his tail instantly sprang out and tickled her to wake her up. She blinked and looked around confused.

"Where was I? What was I saying?"

"You were saying: 'Squirrel Boy and the Black Widow: an amazing team.'"

"Oh yes. Don't you agree? I can't wait for our next adventure," she said.

And neither could he.

THE END

All about Animals Blog

30 May

Update: Squirrel Hunter sentenced!
By Angela Kettle

Great news for all animal lovers! The former Squirrel Hunter, Auberon Steyn, has been found guilty of animal cruelty and sentenced to 200 hours of community service. And this is the best bit: his punishment is to clean out the dung from the elephant enclosure at the zoo, twice a week for the next two years. I've got some news for Auberon Steyn: elephants do an awful lot of poo! And it's extremely smelly! Serves him right!

21 March

The Squirrel Hunter uncovered
Exclusive by Angela Kettle

I can finally reveal the name of the man who has been terrorising squirrels in Grange Park. He is Auberon Steyn, and he is a very, very bad man indeed. I have passed his name on to the RSPCA and the police, and they are investigating.

Now that the Squirrel Hunter has been unmasked, I'm going to concentrate on getting to the bottom of that other mystery: Who is Squirrel Boy?! Watch this space!

Coming soon from a superhero near you…

CHAPTER ONE

Professor Rupert Stinger doesn't look much like a scientist. He doesn't have crazy hair, for instance, or a particularly large forehead. He has a thin face and a neat side parting.

He is a scientist, however: an incredibly clever one. He works at the university, with other brilliant scientists, although none is quite as brilliant as him.

At the weekend, in fact, he had performed a most fantastic experiment in his cellar and, immediately after, he'd emailed the following message to all of his colleagues:

I have made a very great discovery. Join me in the meeting room on Monday morning at 9:00, and I will explain all.

Rupert Stinger

At nine o'clock, all of the scientists were sitting around a large table, waiting for him. There were three women and four men, and only one of them looked like a mad scientist from a book.

Rupert Stinger, buzzing with excitement, strode in, sat down and cleared his throat to get their attention.

"I have invented a machine," he began,

as calmly as he could, "that will completely change the world as we know it, more than any other invention in history."

There were gasps.

"More than the car?" asked one.

"More than the car, and the telephone, and even the computer," said Professor Stinger.

There were more gasps.

"More than the electric popcorn popper?" asked the scientist-who-looked-like-a-scientist.

"Yes," Professor Stinger said, patiently. "Even more than that. My machine..." He paused to increase the anticipation "...can make... hybrid animals!"

But instead of gasps this time, there were mumbles and tuts.

"Hybrid animals already exist," one of the scientists pointed out. "The liger, for example: half-lion, half-tiger."

"Notforgettingthemule,ofcourse,"added another, "half a donkey and half a horse."

"Or the zedonkey: half-zebra, half--donkey," someone else chimed in. "And there are many, many more examples. Hybrids are nothing new. Far from it."

"Ah," said Professor Stinger, putting a finger in the air, "that's all perfectly true. But lions and tigers aren't so very different, are they? They're both big cats. And donkeys, horses and zebras are also very alike. But what my machine can do is make hybrids out of animals that are completely different. For example, a shelephant: a sheep crossed with an elephant. Imagine that! It would completely revolutionise farming! Just think how much wool we'd get!"

He leaned back in his chair, expecting gasps of amazement followed by enthusiastic congratulations. Instead there was complete silence, and a lot of head-shaking.

"What if the machine turned the elephant sheep-sized?" asked one of the scientists eventually. "Then you'd have a sheep with a trunk, which would be very silly."

"And anyway," said another, "elephants would get far too hot if they had a coat of wool. It's a terrible idea."

The scientist-who-looked-like-a-scientist had his hand up.

"You could cross a sheep with a kangaroo,"

he said, "and get a woolly jumper!"

Amid all the groans at the terrible joke, Rupert Stinger ploughed on, more desperately, now:

"How about a 'cog', then? A cow-dog combination. It would give us milk and fetch our slippers."

There was more head-shaking, and everyone was now looking at Rupert Stinger with real pity.

"OK, then," he said, trying one more time. "What about a hybrid of a wolf and a bee? A wee?"

"The man's crazy!" said one scientist.

"Ridiculous!" said another. "He's lost his mind!"

Even the scientist-who-looked-like-a-scientist thought the professor had gone a bit far.

Rupert Stinger, his face turning the colour of beetroot, bowed his head, stood up uneasily and, without looking back, trudged out of the room.

CHAPTER TWO

When the professor usually got home, he liked to sit down and have a nice cup of tea and a biscuit, while flicking through his favourite magazine, *Modern Science*.

But not today. Today he stomped sulkily down the stairs to his cellar so he could be with his machine.

You might think that it looks less like an incredible machine, and more like a small portaloo and a microwave oven, with their doors removed.

To be continued...